DISCARDED

The Show
Must Go On

Adaptation by Jamie White
Based on the TV series teleplays written by
Raye Lankford and Karen Barss
Based on characters created by Susan Meddaugh

HOUGHTON MIFFLIN HARCOURT
Boston · New York · 2012

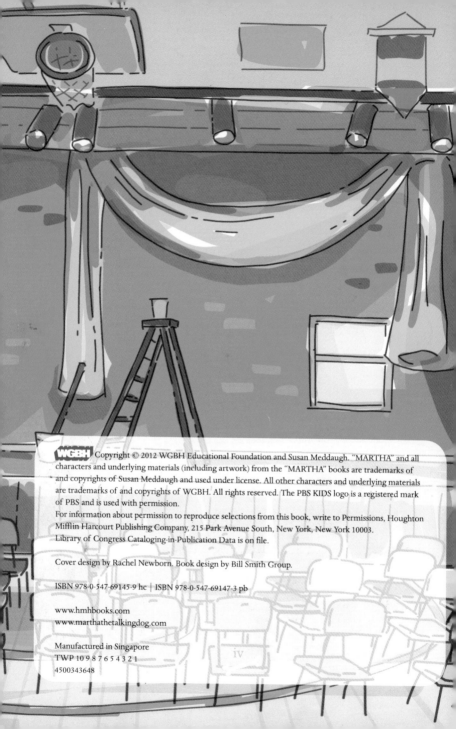

For information about permission to reproduce selections from this book, write to Permissions, Houghton Mifflin Harcourt Publishing Company, 215 Park Avenue South, New York, New York 10003.

Library of Congress Cataloging-in-Publication Data is on file.

Cover design by Rachel Newborn. Book design by Bill Smith Group.

ISBN 978-0-547-69145-9 hc | ISBN 978-0-547-69147-3 pb

www.hmhbooks.com
www.marthathetalkingdog.com

Manufactured in Singapore
TWP 10 9 8 7 6 5 4 3 2 1
4500343648

iv

MARTHA SAYS HELLO

> Ladies and gentlemen,
> boys and girls . . .
> welcome to my book!

We <u>have</u> a <u>wonderful</u> story for you <u>today</u>. You'll <u>laugh</u>. You'll cry. You'll see a dog <u>become</u> a cat. I'm your narrator, Martha the talking dog and world-famous actress.

1

(Okay, I'm only a big woof here in Wagstaff City. But a dog can dream, can't she?)

My person Helen is a pretty good actress herself. Just ask her nervous friend Truman. He discovered her talent when we played in the attic one day. Truman and I huddled in a corner. Someone—or some*thing*—was after us!

"Martha, we're trapped!" Truman whispered. "This is horrible. There might be spiders up here, or bats, or . . . *m-m-m-mold!*"

"Shhh!" I said. "I thought I heard something."

In the shadows, a blanket moved and
something crept toward us. Closer and closer.
Two hands reached out, and—*yikes!*—they
grabbed Truman.

"Got you!" said a
witchy voice.

"Arggh!" Truman
cried. He took off
like a shot, bonked
his head on a beam,
and hit the floor.

I sighed.

Helen stuck her head out from under the
blanket. "Truman?"

He was okay. But you can see why playing
pretend with Truman is not a good idea.
Helen gave him an ice pack and sat him down
in the kitchen.

"You guys!" said Truman. "I was
pretending. But if I were a kid who scared
easily, that would have been *terrifying*. Helen,
you should be an actress. You've got a gift."

"Gift?" I said. "How come she gets a
present and I don't?"

Helen patted my head. "No. Truman means *gift* like when you're naturally good at something. Like being a talking dog."

This was true. Ever since Helen fed me her alphabet soup, I've had the gift of gab. That is, I could speak. And speak and speak . . . No one's sure how or why, but the letters in the soup traveled up to my brain instead of down to my stomach.

Now as long as I eat my daily bowl of alphabet soup, I can talk. To my family— Helen, baby Jake, Mom, Dad, and Skits, who only speaks Dog. To Helen's cousin Carolina and her friends—Truman, T.D., and Alice. To anyone who'll listen.

Sometimes they all wish I didn't talk quite so much. But hey, it's the gift that keeps on giving!

"Helen, you have a gift for being a terrific itch-er of itchy spots," I said as she got to the spot behind my ears. "Ahh!"

"Do you think you might be an actress someday?" Truman asked her.

"No way!" said Helen. "Sign-ups for the school play were this week. I said I'd be a ticket taker."

"Really? What's the play about?" said Truman.

Helen shrugged. "Something science-y. The solar system, I think."

"Don't you want to show off your gift?" I asked.

Helen shook her head. "You're the expert at showing off. I like to stay in the background. Which reminds me: I'm supposed to meet T.D. to paint backdrops for the play. See you later."

She ran out the door, leaving me with an idea. I grabbed the phone book with my mouth and dropped it in front of Truman.

"Will you look up a number for me?" I asked.

I'd decided to give Helen another sort of gift. The present kind. But as you'll see, it would create a whole lot of drama.

Now on with the show—er, story!

ACT ONE

The next morning, Helen was in for a surprise
when she stepped onto the schoolyard.

"Halley! Wait!" called her cousin
Carolina, catching up to her. "No wonder
you're a comet. You're a very fast walker."

"Huh?" said Helen.

"Aren't you excited, Halley?" Carolina asked. "It's excellent casting. Because we're cousins in space, too. I'm a big ball of gas. You're a little ball of gas. See you around the solar system, you little comet, you!"

Then she strutted into school, announcing, "Make way! Star coming through!"

Helen was confused. "We're cousins in space?" she wondered aloud.

Things got weirder inside. She met her friends T.D. and Alice at their lockers.

"Way to go, Halley!" said T.D.

"Halley! Congratulations," said Alice.

"Okay," said Helen. "What's with everyone today? My name is *not* Halley."

"Haven't you seen the cast list yet?" Alice asked.

"Cast list?"

"The all-grades school play. Remember?" asked T.D. "It just went up a few minutes ago, and we're all in it."

Helen's stomach flip-flopped. "There's got to be some mistake. I don't want to be in the play."

AAAAAARGH!

But when she read the list, there she was:

Halley's Comet . . . Helen.

Helen's scream rang down the hallway.

She went to her teacher, Mrs. Clusky, to find out what was going on.

"Don't be modest," said Mrs. Clusky, who was sorting costumes for the play. "Your mother told me you have many talents."

"Talents?" asked Helen.

"All the things you do well. You draw, paint, sing, act. You're very talented. You'll be a superb Halley's Comet!"

"My *mother?*"

Mrs. Clusky nodded, holding the comet costume against Helen. "Yes. She phoned yesterday and said you wanted to be in the play."

"But I don't! I just want to tear tickets!" said Helen, panicked.

"Your mother said you'd say that, and that I shouldn't believe you. She also said to pick up some dog biscuits. The frosted kind."

"But we don't let Martha eat frost—" Then she realized Mom hadn't called at all. It was . . .

Martha!

A SMALL, FROZEN MASS

From the sofa, Skits and I stared at the front door. Helen would be home any minute.

"I can't wait to find out what part Helen got in the play," I said. "She'll be outstanding!"

Woof!

"No, Skits, *outstanding* doesn't mean Helen has to stand outside," I answered. "It means she'll be super duper great."

The door slammed. *Bang!*

Uh-oh.

Helen stomped to her room. I followed.

"I thought you'd be happy," I said. "You'll get to show what an acting expert you are."

"*Expert?*" she cried. "An expert is someone who's really good at something. I've never done a play in my life." She flopped onto her bed and hid her face behind a pillow.

"That doesn't mean you won't be fantastic," I said.

The rest of our family thought so too. When Dad found out, he was excited.

"I tell you, Helen, there's nothing like performing," he said. "And you and Martha are always putting on shows."

"But that's not in front of people. That's just for you and Mom," Helen said.

Dad smiled. "You just need a little practice. You'll get the knack of it!"

So the next day, Helen found herself standing next to Carolina on the school stage.

"I have to get out of this!" Helen said.

Carolina's jaw dropped. "Get out of it? This is your chance to shine! Like your cousin the sun."

"But I don't want to shine. I want to disappear."

Carolina patted Helen's shoulder. "Relax. There's nothing to it. All you do is say your lines and try not to trip on your costume."

Helen was not reassured. Especially after what happened next to Carolina.

Oops!

Helen's jitters grew worse at rehearsal. Standing with Carolina in the wings, she waited for her cue. The other actors were almost done singing:

It was time for Helen to appear.
Only her feet wouldn't budge.

"Helen?" called Mrs. Clusky.
"That's your cue."

"Oops!" said Helen. "Too late."

The actors sang again:

"Haven't seen you in a—!"

This time, Helen burst onto the stage. But the others were still singing.

"Oops! Too early," said Helen.

"Wait for your cue," Mrs. Clusky reminded her. The kids giggled.

The third time, everyone waved Helen onto the stage. In a quiet, quivering voice, she sang her song as fast as she could.

Helen said it was the most embarrassing day of her life.

"I bet you were spectacular," I told her at home.

"Yes," she said. "A spectacular disaster!"

A COMET
IS BORN

Helen was *not* enjoying being Halley's Comet. But I knew she'd be great.

Hey, you know what else are great? Carrots. Really. I drooled as T.D. ate them at the yogurt shop.

"Those look good," I said. (Which means "Feed me" in Martha-speak.)

"Dogs like carrots?" asked T.D.

"I do. It's a gift. I'm an eating machine."

T.D. threw me one. I tried to bite it, but—splurt!—the carrot slipped out of my mouth.

Unexpectedly, Helen joined us. "Martha? You're not begging for food again, are you?"

I'd have answered her, but I had finally bit the carrot. The sweet sound of success filled my ears.

"Uh, no," said T.D. "I'm just full. So, how do you like performing?"

"Ugh! I can't get the knack of it."

Mm . . . tasty!

"Snack?" I said. (It's hard to hear over carrot-crunching.) "Don't mind if I do."

Helen shook her head. "Not snack. *Knack.*"

"Nap? No thanks. I'm not sleepy. But I'm hungry."

"KNACK!" shouted Helen. "Like when you figure out an easy way to do something hard."

T.D. gave me another carrot. *Splurt!* Slippery little guys. "Wish I had a knack for eating carrots," I said. "They keep getting away.

Why don't you order a burger? I'm an expert at eating those."

But Helen's mind was elsewhere. "I'm going to tell Mrs. Clusky I quit."

"You can't give up after only one rehearsal," I said.

"Martha's right," said a voice behind us. It was Carolina. She wrinkled her nose. "I can't believe I just agreed with your dog."

(Hmph. I let that one go.)

After our snacks, Carolina, Helen, and I walked home. "Look, acting is easy," said Carolina.

"Trust me. I'm an expert. This is my seventh school play."

Helen looked doubtful. "Yes, but it's the first time you've had any lines."

"How hard can it be?" said Carolina. "It's pretend! Pretend to be a comet. *Be* that ball of ice and dust. Dust doesn't get nervous."

"But I'm a kid. And I do," said Helen.

Something Carolina had said made me stop. Pretend! Helen and I pretended all the time. "Helen, you don't get nervous when we're pretending at home, do you?" I asked.

"No."

"So what if I come to the rehearsal and I can be your practice audience?"

"I guess," she said.

"Perfect! You can't fail. Because I think everything you do is terrific." To prove it, I gave her a slobbery kiss.

From then on, whenever Helen practiced, I was there to watch. At first, I watched her stumble and stutter. But the more she practiced, the better she got. She danced. She sang. She became the comet.

"Woo-hoo!" I cheered. "You're really getting the knack of this stuff."

Helen practiced at home, too. Skits and I wagged our tails to the beat as she performed.

(Who cares that she kept dancing into walls?)

Woof!

"I agree, Skits!" I said. "Excellent! Outstanding! Superb! Boy, I sure wish I could whistle."

Skits and I leapt across the room to kiss Helen. This comet was definitely ready to fly tomorrow night.

MARTHA LENDS A PAW

It was finally here. The night of the play!

"Don't be nervous," I told Helen. "You're going to be outstanding."

On stage, the actors were doing great. But backstage, Helen couldn't stop pacing. "What if I forget my lines?" she asked. "Or my tail! I forgot my tail!"

I never have that problem.

She ran off to get her comet tail.

"Don't worry! I've got you covered! I know all the lines," I called. I hoped she'd hurry back soon. It was nearly her turn to go on.

As I waited, I looked out into the darkened theater. Somewhere, Mom, Dad, and baby Jake sat out there in the audience.

Unfortunately, the school janitor was much closer.

"Hey!" he said. "What are you doing here? Dogs aren't allowed in school."

He pushed me outside, slamming the door behind me.

"No! Wait!" I cried, scratching at the door.

Helen needs me!

I had to get back in—fast!

Meanwhile, Helen had returned to the wings. Carolina helped Helen put on her comet tail. "I don't know what you're worried about," Carolina said. "You're a superb little actress. You have a gift."

Helen smiled weakly. "Thanks. I wish I had some courage too."

Outside, I was trying to sneak in. I spotted a small open window above a dumpster.

Could I reach it? I leaped on a garbage can . . .
and onto the dumpster . . . and into the
window. *Oof!* And that's where I stopped . . .
stuck . . . halfway in and halfway out.

"Where's Martha?" Helen asked. "They're
almost at my cue."

Carolina shrugged.

"I can't do it without Martha!" Helen looked sick. The actors were coming to the end of their song.

I had to get unstuck! I had to be backstage for Helen! Besides, the smell of the dumpster was making me hungry. I wiggled and pushed and pulled, until at last . . . *POP!* I was back inside.

I raced to the wings just as Helen timidly stepped onto the stage.

In the spotlight, Helen squinted.
She looked out, small and frozen.

Helen! I wanted to shout. *I'm right here.*

She looked around. The actors held
their breath.

C'mon, Helen.

Then she saw me! She smiled
and then she sang. Every word
came out loud
and clear.

That's my person! I thought proudly.

When she was done, the actors lifted Helen into the air. "And now the moment you've been waiting for," they announced. "The star of the solar system—the sun!"

As Helen and the others left the stage, Carolina made her grand entrance.

Alone, she stared out into the crowd. And stared. And, um . . . stared.

Carolina didn't sing. She didn't even move.

"She's got stage fright," T.D. whispered. "Somebody do something!"

The actors all looked at each other. No one knew how to help.

It's always up to the dog, I thought. So, I'll let you in on a little secret.

Hidden in the wings, I sang Carolina's solo for her. I'd been to so many rehearsals, I knew all the words to all the songs.

I'm the Sun, the only one
That's in the solar system.

When I was done, everyone clapped for Carolina. She gave me a secret smile. The whole cast took a bow.

"Bravo!" the audience cheered.

I wished I could clap too. (Oh, to have hands!) But it sure felt good to lend a paw.

My family met outside after the show.

"That was excellent, you two," Dad said, hugging Helen and Carolina. "Aren't you glad you did the play, Helen?"

Helen winced. "It was okay once I got the knack. But that was my farewell performance."

"Carolina, I had no idea you were such an expert actress," Dad said. "You were outstanding."

"I love how you imitated Martha's voice," said Mom. "She does think she's the center of the universe sometimes."

"What I want to know," said Dad, "is how did you talk without moving your lips?"

Carolina patted my head. "I had a lot of help from Martha."

We never told Mom and Dad what happened. And soon it was time for someone else to take center stage. Can you guess who?

INTERMISSION

We're now in the middle of our story. It's time to stretch your legs. Get a drink. Grab a snack. And maybe one for your favorite dog too? (Psst: I like hot dogs.)

ACT TWO

I guess it was only a matter of time before my talent was discovered. I was doing my stand-up routine at the fire hydrant, telling jokes to the gang.

"What's the only thing worse than a cat?" I asked them.

"Two cats!" I said.

The dogs howled with laughter.

That's when I heard Mrs. Boxwood. (She's Alice's mom, and she's very nice. But her son, Ronald, can be pretty grumpy. And what's worse, they have a *cat*—my sneaky archenemy, Nelson.)

"Martha!" Mrs. Boxwood called. "I'm glad I found you! You're just the dog I need. I'm directing a musical at the school and I have a part for you."

"For me?" I asked, wagging my tail.

"Yes, you'll be perfect. I'll send Ronald over with the script. Rehearsals start tomorrow after school. See you then!"

I ran home to share the news with Helen.

"She didn't tell you what the show is?"
Helen asked.

"No, but do you know what this *means?*"

AROO? asked Skits.

I rolled my eyes. "No, it doesn't mean they
can't get anyone else to sign up. It means she
thinks I'm talented. Maybe even a star!
I wonder what she wants me to be."

I could be anything!
I thought. *A witch!*
A happy orphan! Or
a merdog!

I was imagining my neat orange wig
when—*ding-dong!*—the doorbell rang.

"It's him!" I cried. (Who ever thought I'd
be happy to see Ronald?)

Helen opened the door.

"My mother told me to
bring you this," Ronald said,
scowling. He handed Helen
the script.

"Thanks," said Helen.
"Martha can't wait to find out what part
she got."

Ronald's eyes bugged. "Martha?"

"What's the matter?" Helen asked.

"What's wrong with *Nelson*? He should have that part, not her."

"*Nelson*?" asked Helen. "Nelson can't talk. He's just a normal cat."

"A real cat!" said Ronald. "It's totally unfair."

He stomped down the steps. "I'm going to talk to my mom about this."

Nelson? I thought. *This is a musical, not a stinky mewsical. That part, whatever it is, is MINE.*

THE BAD MEWS

"She wants me to play WHAT?" I asked. Mrs. Boxwood had to be joking!

Helen looked through the script. "It's not bad."

"Not bad? It's unheard of!"

"It's *Alice in Wonderland*," said Helen. "The Cheshire Cat is a great part. And you have a song."

"A *cat* song! 'Meow, meow, meow,' "
I mimicked. " 'Everybody look at me. I'm
a cat. I think I'm the boss of the world.' "

"But that's what actors do," said Helen,
pouring herself a glass of milk. "They portray
someone they're not."

"Portray?"

"Yes. *Portray* means to play a part in a play
or movie. The way Carlo portrays a heroic
collie on his TV show, but he's really just a
regular dog."

"At least he plays a dog," I said.

Skits snickered. I didn't see what was

so funny.

"The Cheshire Cat is just a character," said Helen. "A character is a person or animal in a play or book. Actors portray characters that are different from themselves all the time."

I stood my ground.

"Well, I'm sorry. I can't do it. I have principles. This dog will never portray a cat!" I left to tell Mrs. Boxwood just that.

But when I gave Mrs. Boxwood the news, she said, "That's fine, dear."

"Oh," I said, oddly disappointed. "You're agreeing awfully quickly."

"I thought it would be fun, but if you don't want to do it, we'll use Nelson." Mrs. Boxwood turned and called Ronald's name.

"No! Shhh! Wait!" I said. "You want to use *Nelson*? As the Cheshire Cat?"

"Well, he is a cat. Ronald can say his lines from offstage."

"Oh, that won't look good," I said quickly. "Do you think that would look good? I don't think that would look good."

"What is it?" asked Ronald, walking up from behind Mrs. Boxwood.

"Oh, Ronald," she said. "I was just—"

"OKAY, OKAY, I'LL DO IT!" I ran off before I could hear the name "Nelson" again. *Grrr.*

When I returned home, my family looked up from their dinner. "Did you quit the play?" Helen asked.

"Quit? Me?" I asked. *"Never!"*

Skits was snickering again.

BEING THE ENEMY

On the first day of rehearsals, I decided to give it my all. If I was stuck being a cat, then I'd be the coolest cat ever. When Mrs. Boxwood called my name, I bounded on stage.

"Try your song," she said.

I sang with gusto, throwing in some extra
moves to wow her. Like chasing my tail,
rolling over, and playing dead (for drama!).
I ended it all with a show-stopping howl.

AR-OOO!

"Hang on," said Mrs. Boxwood,
silencing the music. "That's a good
start. But you're acting more like a
dog than a cat."

57

"Aww, thanks!" *I'm a natural*, I thought.

"But the character is a cat, remember?" she said.

"But the Cheshire Cat's a cool cat. So maybe he's more like a dog than a cat."

Ronald, who'd been painting a backdrop, hurried to his mom's side. "Nelson knows how to act like a cat. He could do this part."

But Mrs. Boxwood wasn't paying attention to Ronald.

"Martha, if you're going to portray a cat, you need to be very catlike. You have to convince us that you're a cat."

"You don't think if people see a big, singing cat they'll want their money back?" I asked.

"Um, no," she said.

Outside, we talked more after rehearsal. "Try observing cats," she suggested. "Find out what motivates them. Someone's motivation is what makes them act the way they do."

"I know cats. They stink and they're selfish," I said. "They stare into space like zombies. Then, for variety, they yack up a furball on the furniture."

"Listen," said Mrs. Boxwood, kneeling down. "If you're going to portray a cat, you have to understand cat psychology. You must know what cats are thinking and feeling."

After she left, I thought about what she said. What *are* cats thinking?

" 'Ruff, ruff. I'm thirsty. Where's the toilet?' " said a voice behind me.

I turned to see Ronald imitating me to his friends and Nelson. They all laughed. Whatever Nelson was thinking, I didn't want to know.

I met Alice and Helen at the yogurt shop and told them about my day.

"I'll show everyone," I said. "I'll be the best darn cat a dog has ever been."

"I believe you," said Helen.

"You do? I wish I believed me," I said. "How am I ever going to figure out cat psychology? You know, what's going on in their minds? Like what they think or how they feel."

"I don't know about psychology," said Alice, "but I know someone who can teach you to act like a cat."

If she's talking about Nelson, I thought, *I'm in for a cat-astrophe.*

Luckily, Nelson was not the furball who'd be giving me cat lessons. It was my friend Kitten. Even I like kittens. (But please don't tell anybody.)

The kitten pawed at my dog tag.

"No time for fun, Kitten," I said. "I'm here on business," I was ready to think like the enemy. To walk in their paws. To live in their fur. To *be* a cat. (Gah. What I do in the name of art!)

Lesson one: Balancing. The kitten walked along a hose, keeping all four paws in a straight line. This was some fancy feline footwork.

"Okay. Here goes nothing." I stepped up, wobbled, and fell to the ground. "Yipes!"

Next, I learned how to sharpen my claws on a tree. I nailed it.

I learned how to clean my ears with my paws. *Paws*itively easy.

But then came the hard stuff. The kitten jumped up onto the deck's narrow railing. *Meow?*

"You want me to jump up onto *that?*" I asked. Gulp!

Meow! Meow!

"Okay! I'll do it."

After several tries, I scrambled onto the railing.

"I made it! I . . . Whooooooa!"

Cat lessons were officially over.

PRACTICE MAKES PURR-FECT

At the next rehearsal, I came prepared.

A big tree filled the stage. I sat on a top branch. Alice, playing, well, Alice, stood underneath. We practiced our lines.

"What sort of people live here?" she asked.

I pointed with a paw. "In that direction lives a Hatter, and in that direction lives a March Hare. Visit either if you like. They're both mad. And by mad, I mean *crazy*."

"Oh, but I don't want to go among mad people," said Alice.

I climbed down to the stage and sharpened my claws on the tree. "I'm mad, you're mad."

"But how do you know I'm mad?" Alice asked.

Washing my ears just like Kitten, I answered, "You must be, or you wouldn't have come here."

"Wonderful, Martha!" Mrs. Boxwood exclaimed. "You must have been taking lessons."

"Well, I have one friend who's a . . . cat," I said.

"Keep up the good work," said Mrs. Boxwood.

I felt like a star. I floated backstage, where Helen measured me for my costume.

"Was I really okay?" I asked.

"You were great," said Helen.

"Yes, but I want to be *purr*fect."

Suddenly, Ronald's face peeked through the costumes hanging in front of me. "Oh, you'll be perfect, all right," he whispered to himself. "Perfectly ridiculous. Heh, heh."

"Sorry, what did you say?" I asked him.

He blushed. "Um, nothing. Got to run."

Ronald's head disappeared. And yet, for the next few days, I had this funny feeling that he was always lurking somewhere nearby.

Later, Helen and I went to the park with Skits. They played fetch. I played it cool like a cat.

"Martha, are you sure you don't want to play?" Helen asked.

"Cats don't play fetch," I said. "And remember: call me Kitty."

Helen sighed. "Sorry, *Kitty*."

"Until the show opens, I'm one hundred percent cat."

Just then, something appeared in front of me. SQUIRREL! My ears perked up. My legs itched to run. My brain said, *Chase the squirrel!*

Instead, I took a deep breath.

I'm a cat, I said to myself. *I don't chase squirrels. I don't bark. I don't . . . Argh! CHASE THE SQUIRREL! CHASE THE SQUIRREL!*

I couldn't help it. I chased the squirrel.

"I guess some instincts are too strong to control," said Helen when I returned.

"Hey! My stink is under control," I said.

"*Instinct* doesn't mean 'stink,' " said Helen. "An instinct is something you do without ever having to be taught how. Dogs can't resist their instinct to chase squirrels."

After that, I tried harder to be a cat. Starting at the fire hydrant.

Woof! Arf! Yip! my pals greeted me.

I stuck my nose in the air. "I don't talk to smelly, dopey dogs."

The dogs chased me for four blocks. (New cat lesson: Don't visit fire hydrants.)

I stayed in character at home, too. When Helen called me inside, I remained in the backyard, calmly washing my paws.

"Martha!" Helen shouted. "Why aren't you answering me?"

"My name is Kitty," I reminded her.

Helen groaned. *"Kitty, it's time to come in."*

I sat on.

"Now what?" Helen snapped.

"Helen, you know cats don't come when they're called."

"MARTHA!"

"Okay, okay, I'm coming." *Stars need their rest anyway,* I thought. *After all, tomorrow is the big night!*

THE CRAZIEST CAT

In the school auditorium, the audience murmured excitedly.

Mrs. Boxwood had gathered the cast backstage. "Everyone ready?" she asked. "Break a leg!"

The lights went down. The curtain
rose. Showtime!

Mrs. Boxwood narrated. "Alice followed the
white rabbit down the rabbit hole. She found
herself falling and falling."

Alice really looked like she was falling,
thanks to a moving backdrop powered by
T.D. on a stationary bike.

Backstage, Helen helped me with my costume. Not long ago, I was helping her. Now I knew why she'd felt so nervous as Halley's Comet.

"I hope I don't forget my lines," I worried.

"You'll be great," she said. "You've rehearsed it a hundred times. What could go wrong?"

We hardly paid attention to Ronald, or we might have had an idea.

Just then, I sniffed a familiar smell. "Hmm. That's funny."

"What?" asked Helen.

"I thought I smelled a . . . Never mind. Just nerves, I guess."

"Martha!" Mrs. Boxwood whispered. "Get ready. You're almost on."

I walked onto the stage. It looked like a storybook forest. I climbed up onto my branch and waited.

Soon Alice appeared below. "Oh, where am I?" she asked. "If I only knew which direction to go."

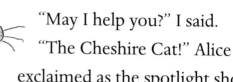

"May I help you?" I said.

"The Cheshire Cat!" Alice exclaimed as the spotlight shone on me. "Can you tell me which way I ought to go from here?"

"That depends on where you want to get to."

"I don't care much where," she replied.

"Then it doesn't matter which way you go," I said.

The audience cracked up. It felt great!

Ronald and Nelson watched from the wings. Ronald, dressed as a playing card, was holding a box. I didn't remember that from rehearsal. Hmm. What was he up to?

Alice continued, "How do you know
you're mad?"

I moved next to her to sing, *"Cats are crazy.
We're all mad! And you can take it from me . . ."*

"Watch this, Nelson," Ronald whispered
as I sang. He tapped his head. "This is
using psychology."

He opened the box.
Something furry shot out
of it and across the stage.
It was a . . . SQUIRREL!

THE SHOW MUST GO ON

I watched the squirrel scurry toward me. Ronald gave me a sneaky smile, and I knew he was sure I would chase it.

But then, something incredible happened. The squirrel made a U-turn and ran . . . right up Ronald's pant leg!

"Ay-yi-YI!" Ronald hopped on one foot across the stage, shaking his leg wildly. "GET IT OUT! GET IT OUT!"

It looked like he'd made up his own dance. He did his crazy squirrel boogie smack into a tree. *Tim-ber!*

The audience roared.

All around me, scenery toppled. It was chaos.

Finally the squirrel scooted out of Ronald's pants and ran across the stage.

I stopped singing, but if Ronald wanted me to chase that squirrel and ruin the play, he was barking up the wrong tree.

"Too bad I'm not a dog," I said to Alice. "I'd love to chase that. Now where were we?" I said.

"Because the Cheshire Cat is the craziest cat there ever was! Woo!"

The crowd went wild.

After the play, Helen and I had a good laugh. Our acting experiences had taught us a lot. Helen learned that with practice, she can do anything. And I learned that although I can portray a pretty convincing cat, there's nothing I'd rather be than a dog. Especially a talking dog!

Hey, you know what? You've come to the end of my story. You've read the whole book. Take a bow.

Outstanding! Woo hoo! (You'd hear clapping right now, if I had hands.) Bravo!

The End.

GLOSSARY

How many words do you remember from the story?

character: a person or animal in a play or book.

expert: someone who's really good at something.

gift: a natural ability or a present (because having a natural ability is like getting one).

instinct: something one does without ever having to be taught how.

knack: an easy way to do something hard.

motivation: what makes someone act the way they do.

outstanding: superduper great.

portray: to play a part in a play or movie.

psychology: what goes on in someone's mind, like what one thinks or how one feels.

talent: a special skill.

Martha Says, "Break a Leg"

Do you have a talent? Maybe a gift for singing or a knack for acting? You don't need to wait for a school play to perform. You can put on a show in your own backyard. Martha, the acting expert, has a few ideas to get you started.

Set the Scene

You don't need a real theatre to set the stage for drama. Household items can be used to create scenery, costumes, and props. Get creative by drawing or painting scenery for your play. Look through your closet to find costume elements. And search through your toys for just the right props. Can't find what you're looking for? Then just pretend—that's what acting is all about anyway!

Martha's Theater

Sometimes actors read a story aloud as their performance. Pick a chapter from this book that has lots of dialogue. Cast your friends to portray the narrator and characters.

Play in a Bag

Gather different costumes and props in a bag. With your friends, open the bag and make up words and actions on the spot using the items you find. Create your own characters. To be outstanding, discover your character's psychology and motivation.

Another Kind of Skits

Skits is not just the name of Helen's nontalking dog. Skits are also short theatrical sketches that are usually silly. Write a skit about something funny that's happened to you. Act it out with friends. Can you ignore your instinct to laugh?